DANIEL TIGER'S NEIGHBORHOOD

MW00902753

Daniel's First Airplane Ride

By Haley Hoffman
Poses and layouts by Jason Fruchter

SIMON SPOTLIGHT
An imprint of Simon & Schuster Children's Publishing Division • New York London Toronto Sydney New Delhi
1230 Avenue of the Americas, New York, New York 10020
This Simon Spotlight paperback edition May 2024 • © 2024 The Fred Rogers Company
Simon & Schuster: Celebrating 100 Years of Publishing in 2024
For information about special discounts for bulk purchases, please contact Simon & Schuster Special Sales
at 1-866-506-1949 or business@simonandschuster.com. • Manufactured in the United States of America 0824 LAK
10 9 8 7 6 5 4 3 2 • ISBN 978-1-6659-5199-9 • ISBN 978-1-6659-5200-2 (ebook)

The Tiger family is going on a special trip far away. "I'm going to fly on an airplane for the first time!" says Daniel.

Daniel packs Tigey in his backpack while his parents pack their suitcases. Daniel asks his dad what happens on an airplane trip.

Dad Tiger sings,

"When we do something new,
let's talk about what we'll do!"

Dad Tiger explains to Daniel that Trolley will drive them to the airport. First they'll get their tickets. Then they'll go to the check-in counter to leave their bags.

Next they'll go through a security checkpoint to make sure only safe things go on the plane. Then they'll find the gate where they will wait for their airplane!

Dad Tiger picks up Daniel's toy airplane and shows Daniel how the plane will take off and fly into the air. "That looks tigertastic!" says Daniel.

Soon the Tiger family is ready for their trip!
"Yay!" Margaret cheers.
They ride Trolley and sing,

"We're on our way to the airport, for a special airplane trip!
Won't you fly along with me?
♪ ♪ *Won't you fly along with me?"* ♪ ♪

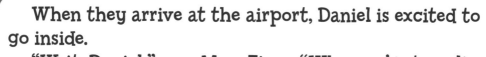

When they arrive at the airport, Daniel is excited to go inside.

"Wait, Daniel," says Mom Tiger. "When we're traveling, especially when we're someplace new, we need to hold hands so we stay together."

There are a lot of people inside the airport. "It is so crowded," says Daniel.

"There are lots of travelers today," says Dad Tiger.

"I'm feeling a little two stripes nervous," says Daniel. Dad sings,

♪ ♪ *"Grown-ups are here to take care of you."* ♪ ♪

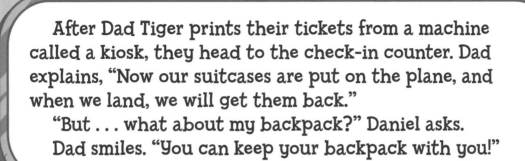

After Dad Tiger prints their tickets from a machine called a kiosk, they head to the check-in counter. Dad explains, "Now our suitcases are put on the plane, and when we land, we will get them back."

"But . . . what about my backpack?" Daniel asks.

Dad smiles. "You can keep your backpack with you!"

Check-In

Next they head toward the security checkpoint. They place their personal belongings on a conveyor belt. Daniel sees his mom and dad taking off their shoes. "Why are you taking off your shoes?" he asks.

Dad explains, "This is another way people at the airport make things safe for the airplane ride. When you're older, you'll take off your shoes too, but for now you can keep them on."

Daniel follows his parents through a metal detector. Dad explains that the metal detector and X-ray machines make sure only safe things are brought onto the plane. After they pass through it, Daniel gets his backpack back, and his parents put on their shoes.

"Where do we go now?" Daniel asks.

"We need to find the gate where we will wait for our airplane," says Mom. She looks up at a big board with lots of numbers on it. "Our airplane will be at this gate. Let's go, my Tiger family!"

10:34

✈ DEPARTURES

		C12	∿
08:52	∿ ∿	A10	∿
09:05	∿	B09	∿
10:20	∿	C42	∿
10:28	∿	B10	∿
11:02	∿	D12	∿
11:35	∿	A19	∿
12:40	∿	B14	∿
01:05	∿		

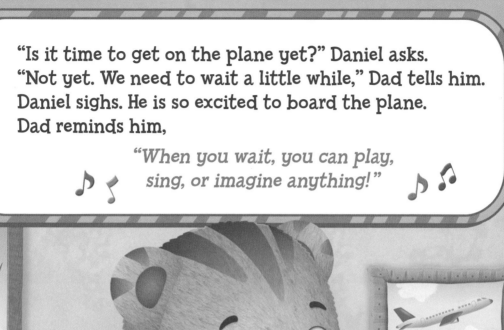

"Is it time to get on the plane yet?" Daniel asks.
"Not yet. We need to wait a little while," Dad tells him.
Daniel sighs. He is so excited to board the plane.
Dad reminds him,

"When you wait, you can play,
sing, or imagine anything!"

"Let's play 'Tigey Says' and practice some of the things we'll do on our airplane ride!" Mom Tiger suggests. "Tigey says . . . let's sit in our seats!" says Mom.

The Tigers stand up and then sit back down in their seats.

"Tigey says . . . show me calm feet. You'll need those on the plane!" Mom Tiger tells everyone.

The gate attendant announces over the loudspeaker that it is time to board the plane. Daniel holds his mom's hand and says, "I have my backpack, Tigey . . . and your hand!" Then the Tigers walk through a jet bridge to board the plane. A flight attendant is there to greet them.

"This is like a tunnel to the plane!" says Daniel.

The Tiger family head to their seats.. Daniel gets to sit next to the window. Margaret sits on Mom's lap. Daniel is so excited he wiggles and kicks his feet. Dad reminds Daniel that he needs to have calm feet on the plane since there are other people around them. Dad sings,

"Give a squeeze nice and slow.
Take a deep breath,
and let it go."

Before the plane is ready for takeoff, the flight attendants explain the safety rules of the plane. They point to a sign on the plane with an image of a seat belt. They explain that when the "fasten seat belt" sign is on, everyone should remain in their seats.

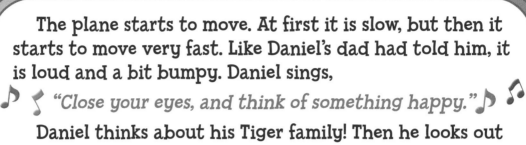

The plane starts to move. At first it is slow, but then it starts to move very fast. Like Daniel's dad had told him, it is loud and a bit bumpy. Daniel sings,

♪ ♪ *"Close your eyes, and think of something happy."* ♪ ♪

Daniel thinks about his Tiger family! Then he looks out the window. "Look, Margaret! We are flying in the air! The Neighborhood looks teeny-tiny!" says Daniel.

A little while later, Daniel starts to wiggle in his seat. "Daniel, do you need to go potty?" Mom Tiger asks. "Yes," says Daniel. He has never been on an airplane potty. Mom sings,

 "When you need to go potty someplace new, you can use a different bathroom."

Dad explains they can get up and use the potty because the "fasten seat belt" sign isn't lit.

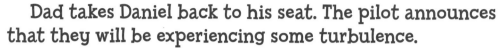

Dad takes Daniel back to his seat. The pilot announces that they will be experiencing some turbulence.

"What's turbulence?" asks Daniel.

"Turbulence is when the plane ride gets a little bumpy, like I told you might happen. But the pilots know what to do to keep us safe," says Dad. He sings,

"When something is new, holding a hand can help you."

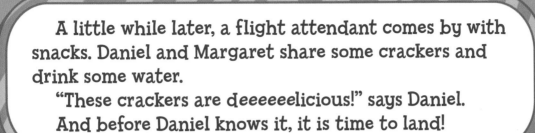

A little while later, a flight attendant comes by with snacks. Daniel and Margaret share some crackers and drink some water.

"These crackers are deeeeeelicious!" says Daniel.

And before Daniel knows it, it is time to land!

When the Tiger family gets off the plane, they are at a new airport! They walk to a special place where they wait for their bags called baggage claim.

Daniel watches as bags go around and around until he spots theirs. "I see them, Mom!" says Daniel.

Daniel and his family head out of the airport. "Flying on an airplane with my family today was grr-ific!" Daniel says. "There are so many things to do and see when you're on a trip with your family. And Mom, Dad, the flight attendants, and the pilots made me feel so safe. Ugga Mugga!"

Hi, neighbor! Here are some words that will help explain what happens when you take a trip on an airplane!

Flight Attendant:
A flight attendant helps keep you safe on the airplane. Flight attendants do a safety demonstration to show you everything you need to know about staying safe on the airplane. They also keep you comfortable by serving drinks and snacks during the trip.

Gate Attendant:
This person checks your ticket before you board the airplane.

Jet Bridge:
This is a hallway that connects the gate to the airplane. You may walk across this when you enter and exit the plane.

Kiosk:
This is a machine that you may use to check in to your flight and print your tickets.

Pilot:
The pilot is the person who flies the airplane. On each plane, there is a pilot and a copilot, who also helps fly the plane.

Security Checkpoints:
Passengers walk through security checkpoints to make sure that only safe items are brought onto the airplane. These checkpoints include X-ray machines and metal detectors.

Turbulence:
This is what it's called when the plane ride feels bumpy. During turbulence, the pilots and flight attendants will ask you to put on your seat belt to help keep you safe.